Shooting Stars Soccer Team

By YoeongAh Kim

Illustrated by HyeongJin Lee

Language Arts Consultant: Joy Cowley

NORWOOD HOUSE PRESS

Chicago, Illinois

DEAR CAREGIVER   MySELF ▌▐▌ Bookshelf is a series of books that support children's social emotional learning. SEL has been proven to promote not only the development of self-awareness, responsibility, and positive relationships, but also academic achievement.

Current research reveals that the part of the brain that manages emotion is directly connected to the part of the brain that is used in cognitive tasks, such as: problem solving, logic, reasoning, and critical thinking—all of which are at the heart of learning.

SEL is also directly linked to what are referred to as 21st Century Skills: collaboration, communication, creativity, and critical thinking. MySELF Bookshelf offers an early start that will help children build the competencies for success in school and life.

In these delightful books, young children practice early reading skills while learning how to manage their own feelings and how to be considerate of other perspectives. Each book focuses on aspects of SEL that help children develop social competence that will benefit them in their relationships with others as well as in their school success. The charming characters in the stories model positive traits such as: responsibility, goal setting, determination, patience, and celebrating differences. At the end of each story, you will find a letter that highlights the positive traits and an activity or discussion to help your child apply SEL to his or her own life.

Above all, the most important part of the reading experience is to have fun and enjoy it!

Sincerely,

Shannon Cannon

Shannon Cannon, Ph.D.
Literacy and SEL Consultant

Norwood House Press • P.O. Box 316598 • Chicago, Illinois 60631
For more information about Norwood House Press please visit our website at www.norwoodhousepress.com or call 866-565-2900.

Shannon Cannon—Literacy and SEL Consultant
Joy Cowley—English Language Arts Consultant
Mary Lindeen—Consulting Editor

Library of Congress Cataloging-in-Publication Data
    Kim, Yoeongah.
    The Shooting Stars soccer team / by YoeongAh Kim ; illustrated by HyeongJin Lee.
        pages cm. -- (Myself bookshelf)
    Summary: "Zebra is happy to join the Shooting Stars Soccer team. The trouble begins when he does not learn the rules and makes mistakes as a result, upsetting the rest of the team. With the help of the coach, Zebra learns from his mistakes and continues to play on the Soccer team"--Provided by publisher.
    ISBN 978-1-59953-648-4 (library edition : alk. paper) -- ISBN 978-1-60357-670-3 (ebook) [1. Soccer--Fiction. 2. Teamwork (Sports)--Fiction. 3. Patience--Fiction. 4. Zebras--Fiction.] I. Lee, Hyeongjin, illustrator. II. Title.
    PZ7.K55998Sho 2014
    [E]--dc23
                                        2014009402

Manufactured in the United States of America in Stevens Point, Wisconsin.
252N—072014

Zebra ran very well.
He also kicked very well.
Captain Lion saw Zebra
and said to him,
"Would you like to join
the Shooting Stars soccer team?"

"Yes, yes!" cried Zebra.
"I'd love to join!"

So Zebra became a soccer player.
Although he could kick and run,
he didn't know how to play soccer.

"Oh, who cares!" he said.
"I just have to kick the ball
into the goal. I will be fine!"

Shooting Stars
Soccer Team

Soon there was a game
between the Shooting Stars soccer team
and the Cyclones soccer team.

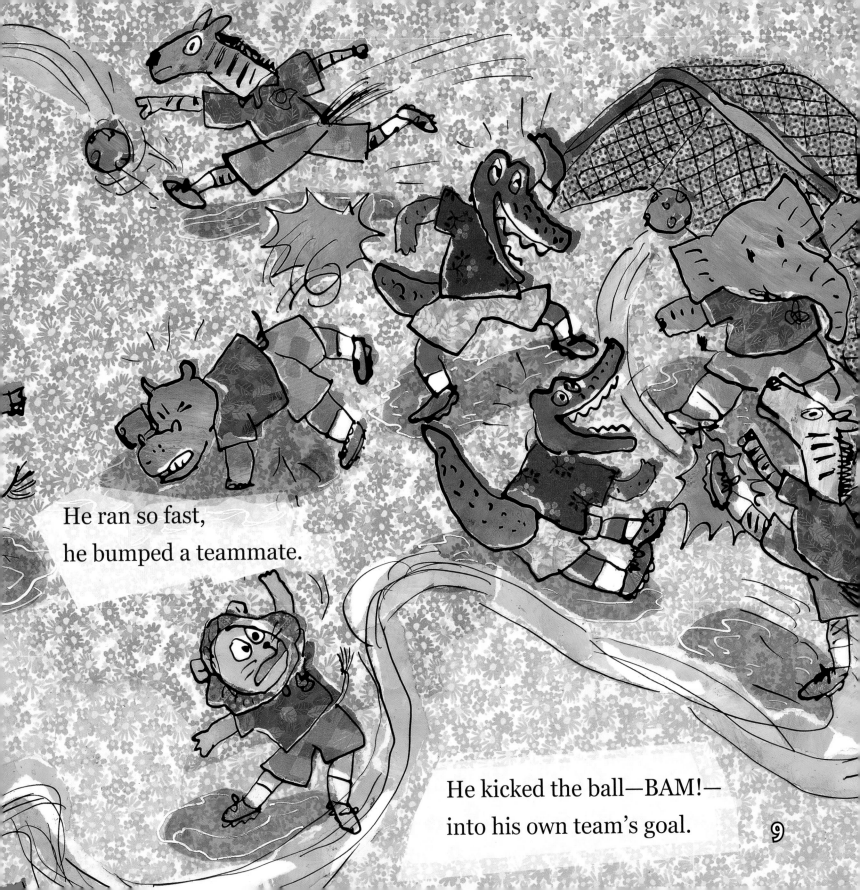

He ran so fast,
he bumped a teammate.

He kicked the ball—BAM!—
into his own team's goal.

9

The Shooting Stars soccer team lost 5 to 0.
"It's the first time we've played badly,"
one of the players said.

But Zebra was excited!
"I scored a goal!" he said.

The players were angry.

"It's Zebra's fault we lost today!"

"He wanted the ball for himself."

"He doesn't know how to play soccer."

From then on,
the Shooting Stars soccer team
ignored Zebra.
They practiced without him.

Captain Lion spoke to the players.
"Don't leave Zebra out. Talk to him.
Tell him what he did wrong."

The other players shrugged.
"Even if we told him,
would he listen to us?"

17

Captain Lion did not give up.
He made every player sit down
to watch a video of the last game.

18

"Let's see how we can play
a better game," he said
as he switched on the video.

19

When Zebra bumped his teammate,
Captain Lion said, "Zebra, you run fast,
but you shouldn't do that to your friends."

"Sorry," said Zebra, "I didn't know that."

When Zebra took the ball from his teammate, Captain Lion said, "Soccer is played by a team. Everyone works together on a team."

Zebra hung his head. "Sorry."

"Look at that!" said Captain Lion.
"You shouldn't kick the ball
into your own team's goal."

Zebra was very embarrassed.
"Now I know why you are angry.
I suppose you don't want me
on the Shooting Stars team."

23

The players gathered around Zebra.

"What are you saying?

We all belong on the team.

Let's give it one more try."

"Oh, thank you!" said Zebra.

From then on,
Zebra worked hard.

He ran fast and kicked the ball hard.
He also passed the ball,
and he helped his teammates
score goals.

Soon there was another match
between the Shooting Stars soccer team
and the Cyclones soccer team.

28

Zebra remembered Captain Lion's words.
Soccer was played by a team.
Everyone needed to work together.

29

BAM!

The Shooting Stars team
scored a fantastic goal.
It was not Zebra's goal,
but he was very happy
because he had helped
a teammate make the point.
Zebra knew what it meant
to be a part of the team.

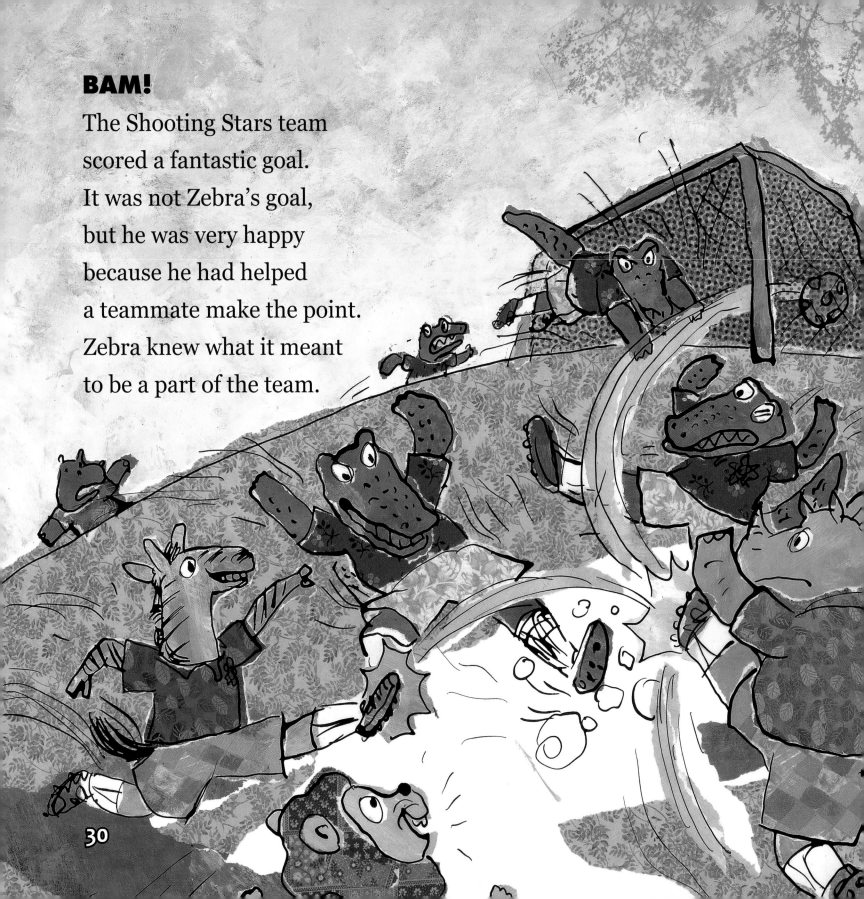